SET FREE

AN ANTHOLOGY

WRITERS FROM
THE PRIORY SCHOOL

SET FREE

AN ANTHOLOGY

Writers From
The Priory School, Hitchin

Content compiled for publication by
Richard Mayers of *Burton Mayers Books*.
Edited *by* Harriet Lacey*, The Priory School*
Cover design by Richard Mayers

First published by Burton Mayers Books 2022.
All rights reserved.

A CIP catalogue record for this book is available from the British
Library

ISBN: 978-1-8384845-2-1

Typeset in **Garamond**

www.BurtonMayersBooks.com

DEDICATION

Set Free is dedicated to the many young readers and writers in the UK and around the world, many of whom have faced mental and physical challenges since the global pandemic hit in 2021 and locked down societies around the world. In particular, these stories reflect the experiences of students who suddenly found themselves kept at home and unable to connect physically with other students except through cyberspace. Even throughout the writing process of this anthology, uncertainties have remained, however the resilience of this generation is a testament to the strength of the human character and the stories based around the theme of breaking free could not be more apt for 2022 and beyond.

~ **CONTENTS** ~

ACKNOWLEDGMENTS

Many thanks to the teachers and parents who have supported their children throughout lockdowns and uncertainty during the academic year.
A special thanks to the readers and writers who supported the project, and the young writers who didn't submit their stories for publishing this time round; we are certain that you will continue to grow in confidence.

Thanks to the business manager, Tony Foster, and Geraint Edwards, Headteacher, who have allowed us to run this project, and to Katie Dolling and Meike Perkins who lead the English department and library respectively, and are proud of what we have done to foster a love of reading and writing at The Priory School, Hitchin.

"I am no bird; and no net ensnares me: I am a free human being with an independent will."

— Charlotte Brontë, Jane Eyre

PRELUDE

By Samuel Benedick

Outside the world was desolate.

It is a bizarre feeling, especially when you live beside a - usually quite busy - main road. I had complained for as long as I can remember about the noisy cars and their revving engines, but now I almost missed them. And although nature seemed to be thriving, my social life was not. How I longed to go outside with my friends. What I would give for a life without covid-19.

I had almost forgotten what it was like to be free.

Lunchtime meant no more online lessons for 1 hour. A time where I'd usually be playing with my friends. On that day however I simply stared at the wall.

Eventually, I turned the TV on only to find Boris Johnson giving another daily briefing. I was about to change the channel until I saw the number of infections and deaths move steadily along the bottom of the screen. My eyes widened as I felt a chilling coldness begin to take over my body. I gasped as the news began to sink in. It reiterated over and over in my ears.

I changed the channel.

From then on I have stopped watching the news, however it seems that not knowing the rate of infections only makes it worse; one day there would be a few hundred infections and the next there would be a few thousand.

Each day was filled with uncertainty and worry.

That is where I began to miss pre-covid times. The times

where I was free.

I began to realise how much I had taken for granted and how much I should have been more grateful for: going to the cinema, seeing my friends, and even getting haircuts, which I once dreaded.

These were all things I began to miss.

I tried to look for the good in things. I really did. I looked to the sun for the slightest ray of joy but even the sun seemed to mock me.

I wondered when I would be set free.

DESTINY

By Phoebe Lally

Foreign is not a word I like to use. It seems rude and disrespectful. If someone is foreign, they are from somewhere other than where you live and that makes them different. Although I guess to Bliss, I am.

Bliss is my... I do not really know what she is. I think the only description for her is the core of my collection, for she really is different to anything I have ever seen. I do not think the full multitude of landscape pictures on Google even give her justice. She is full of high mountains with scooped, flowing valleys; cyan seas with all kinds of marvellous beings filling them and hot, arid places where you burn within minutes. Really, the only bad thing about her is that a large amount of her species are destroying her. Ripping her layer by layer and roasting her slowly on a spit.

One day they will discover how to move habitats and will find another place to live - probably Happrio - and they will eventually destroy my entire collection until they reach extinction. I feel very sorry for them really. Maybe one day they will work out how to solve it but until that day, I am stuck watching them destroy their home, the place I call Bliss. And nothing destroys my favourite part of my collection.

None of my friends have ever had this problem with any of their collections. And none of my others - let's call them planets, I have always liked that name - have ever had anything happen to them either.

Happrio once had inhabitants. They were extremely different from Bliss' and they would sit enjoying the heat until one day a dust storm and a volcano wiped them all out. It was a pity really. I enjoyed having something new to philosophise over.

Bliss' inhabitants keep attempting to work out if there were inhabitants on Happrio. It is taking them ages. Their idiocy seems so obvious to me. Tiny and boastful, they wreck their economy and dignity by leaving the poor to suffer and taking so long to accept each other's feelings about one another.

The only good thing I have started to notice is a sort of campaign that one of them started. They are beginning to raise awareness about the destruction of Bliss. Action is slowly building to help save her; hope ripples out of them and one of them seems to have galvanised all of them into action. Every second, a new person gains awareness and the whole species makes progress.

But, as with any good thing, there is a major downfall: time. They just aren't moving fast enough. There is no way they will succeed in saving Bliss before she is completely destroyed.

I am left with only one option.

Immediately, I set to work on the task of working out how the situation can be resolved without creating too much excitement or probing. To achieve this, I need to transport the inhabitants to another planet while they are asleep, allowing no suspicion to be aroused. As they have already done much research on Happrio and should be able to create sufficient living conditions there, I conclude that he would be the best option. Fortunately, he is right next to Bliss and therefore it will not be too much of a hindrance to transfer them.

The sooner the inhabitants are moved, the sooner Bliss can begin to rehabilitate.

Tonight is the night. As they all shift into silence, my

heart begins to beat uncontrollably. I slowly wave my hands and cause Bliss to glide closer to Happrio. Now for the magic. All my effort collects and Bliss' inhabitants begin to levitate. My face is tied in an expression of struggle and concentration and the beads of sweat gather and begin to pour like waterfalls as I gently lower the creatures onto Happrio.

I collapse.

Relief swirls and whirls about the galaxy and I realise that although it is only one small act in a world of millions, I have just done something unimaginable.

I set Bliss free.

PICKLE

By Eryn Gemmell

I was walking home from school with my best friend. We had our bags slung over our shoulders and could see the sun, low in the sky, just above the houses and the treetops. As we were in different classes, we were talking about what lessons we had that day.

As we turned the corner and onto our road, our conversation was interrupted by a high pitched squawking, coming from behind a bush and on someone's driveway. We saw a beautiful black cat, which had bright emerald green eyes and something small squirming in its mouth. We took a short glance at each other and dropped our bags on the floor, springing into action. I crouched beside the cat and stroked it until it released a small bird, which hurriedly hopped away into the bush. The black cat walked in a circle around the driveway and sat on the floor watching as I looked in the bush for the bird. I heard my friend, Bea, call from the other side of the bush, "Can you see it?" she said, "I can't find it."

"I can't see it either…" I replied, standing up and joining her on the other side of the bush. We shared a concerned look…

We stood back and observed the cat, who was prowling back and forth. We tried to find a nest but couldn't. Turning back to the cat, we saw the bird jump out from under the bush and watched in horror as the cat pounced and caught the bird. Luckily, it dropped the chick as Bea crouched beside it and it gave me the chance to pick the bird up off the floor. We left the cat and took the bird back to my house where we had a better look at it.

The bird had still only got fluff on its head but it seemed eager to fly. I looked further and saw its wing feathers had in fact grown in but were torn in places, some feathers were plucked out and others were cut in half. There was a small amount of blood too, where its wing had been cut but luckily, it seemed that it was not too bad. Bea filled a bowl of warm water and a cloth, which we used to clean the wounds. Then we fed it crushed mealworms through a pipette. We debated on what we should name the bird but eventually I gave in and let Bea name the bird Pickle the Baby Blue Tit, but just Pickle for short.

We would look after Pickle on alternate days. I would carry him round to Bea's house, so she could look after him for the night and then she would carry Pickle back to my house the next day after school. Eventually, he rebuilt his strength. After just a few days, his wounds had healed and after a week his feathers had all grown in, and the broken and torn ones were replaced. Another week quickly passed and Pickle had started to flap his wings and jump as if he was trying to fly, so Bea and I would encourage him to fly between us and land on each of our hands, where he would receive a treat, such as a mealworm, a small piece of bread or a piece of strawberry.

Bea and I loved Pickle so much that we didn't want to let him go. When he was healthy, our parents tried their best to convince us to let him go. We realised he needed more space and more freedom that we could ever provide him with. We agreed to let him go the next day.

In the morning, I entered my kitchen and went to collect Pickle before we set him free. Pickle was not on his small perch, instead he was cold and still in the corner of his box. I gasped in fear, pulling my phone out of my pocket to call Bea and tell her the bad news.

She ran to my house. On seeing the cage, Bea gently picked Pickle up. With tears streaming down her face, she whispered, "He's free."

EAGLE EYES

By Chloe Phillips

He rose from the crisp white pressed sheets of his bed. Rubbing his weary eyes, he tried to focus on his surroundings. He reached across the spotlessly clean square table, and tapped the holographic watch, positioned in the holder; the blue screen glowed dimly, 4:15 am. Sighing heavily, he swung his legs off the edge of his bunk and stumbled out of bed. 'Oh sh-', he whimpered, as his leg made swift contact with the sharp steel corner. Despite the minor injury, he maintained composure, not wanting past events to reoccur. It didn't take much in the 53rd Base for your contract to be revoked. He had only once narrowly escaped termination of his contract, and once was enough. He had worked long and hard to land a position at this biome, working with such senior technologists.

Leaning against the slate sink edge, he sleepily peered at his reflection in the mirror ahead, his ice blue eyes glazed over with tiredness. Touching the glow of the sensor pad with his palm, the lights changed from the usual dim crimson spotlights to the brilliantly illuminated white ceiling panels. He stood still patiently waiting, and a hand-sized door slid smoothly open in the marbled wall, displaying the morning's small vial. Swiftly he grasped it, tipping the entire purple contents in one motion into his mouth. Moments later, he moved differently as he vacated the bathroom, taking confident energised strides back into his room. It usually worked quickly, filling his body with a newfound energy and strength. Feeling ready to commence his day, he flicked his watch on his wrist and checked the programmed routine. After dressing in his smart white uniform, he exited his quarters.

His shoe touched the glossy tiled floor in the hallway, which triggered the activation sensors and lit the exact pathway to his destination. His watch beeped, indicating he was 45 seconds behind schedule; he hastily joined the formation of other identical workers. He placed his wrist on the door marked "D1T7", which sprung to life, swiftly letting him enter. He glanced politely at his co-workers before settling down near a panel of intricate buttons and continuing from where he left. The otherwise quiet room was filled with the continuous tapping from the rows upon rows of workstations. All heads rose from their stooped studious focus, when the woman's shrill voice was heard talking to the guards. He hesitated before softly shifting in his chair and peering across the unit to witness the tense situation. His much older co-workers had already resumed their duties, but they all paid slightly more attention to the voices than their work.

"Yes, yes I understand, but I was only slightly late, a few minutes at most!" The woman talked loudly, surprising even the highly trained guard.

"I was just held up in my quarters, that's all. Can I go now and get on with my work!?"

The guard said nothing. Two more guards marched up either side of her, their steady hands rested on their holstered weapons, their dull blue suits showing they were new recruits. The head guard steadily strode towards the commotion, eyeing the stocky, shorthaired woman with disdain. His sleek black helmet had become illuminated with a red glow. Upon seeing the unnerving red halo, the room of workers quickly busied themselves more fervently with their work. His gloved hand forcefully grabbed her arm in a vice-like grip, and wrenching her hand close to him, he inputted a code into her watch before she could protest. The display screen brightened, and a small message appeared for her eyes only. Her remorseful face softened as she read and she apologised for the fuss she had caused, knowing it was futile to continue in this manner.

A deep gravelly voice emanated from the helmet, "Do you understand what you have read?"

She sighed heavily, disappointed with her actions. "Yes of course".

"Follow me", he sternly directed.

The head guard and the woman's footsteps slowly faded away as they calmly walked towards the lift leading to the basement level.

He paused and an unsettled worrying feeling rushed over him. He knew what the standard code was for insolence of that magnitude, he had never cared about such things before, so why now did her punishment seem uncalled for? His unease lingered, as if taunting him with its confining presence. An unassumingly small technologist with a kind face glanced up from her panel; her eyes met his, which were narrowed with concentration. Seeing his furrowed brow and tensed fists, she leant forward to say something. Before she began speaking, she was distracted by the repetitive beeping sound resonating from the watches on every wrist in the room, reminding them all to take their next dose. They all clinked the bottles together, like they saw happen in old films, and unquestioningly swallowed the purple contents. Noticing that it was time to return to his quarters, he followed the pathway to his room and laid down to rest. His mind pondered the day's events and details that not long ago seemed all consuming, somehow now felt insignificant. With relative ease, he closed his eyes and drifted out of consciousness.

~

I opened my eyes, the unyielding midday sun blazed relentlessly, forcing me to move on in search of shade. I hopped through the undergrowth, feeling the tall green grasses brushing my wingtips as my pace quickened. Catching a little of the warm breeze, I pushed forth from

*the ground and stretched out my wings to full extension to take flight.
I glided through air, experiencing this newfound sense of nothingness.
Climbing higher and higher, my wings sliced through the air. I gazed
at the wide expanse below me and at last felt peace…*

~

Gasping for air, he jolted upright, beads of sweat trickled
down his face. Reaching for his water on the nearby table,
he drank with a sense of urgency, in an attempt to cool the
feverish waves flowing through him. He stared, wide-eyed
at his shaking featherless hands. He saw glimpses of bright
images, like shards of light piercing into the dark, existing
only in sudden disjointed flashes. Rising from the bed, he
moved unsteadily to the sink and drenched his flushed face
in water.

Something felt different.

He scrutinised his reflection, staring intently into his
eyes. He noticed something strange, the once cool
unspoiled blue, was now marred by yellow flecks. He craned
his body forwards so that his nose touched the surface of
the mirror and he stared deep into the eye, following its
movements up, down, left and right. He reached for his
towel and rubbed at the imperfection over and over again,
but to no avail, his reflection still revealed a new imperfect
version of himself. His watch beeped a single warning, and
he stepped away from the mirror. He felt on edge and more
aware of his surroundings. The electrical humming from the
panel lighting surrounded him, and as the lighting changed
(as it did every day at this exact time); today the light seemed
too bright to bear; illuminating the stark reality surrounding
him.

He knew he shouldn't still be in his quarters, but despite
his unforgiving room, the thought of leaving this place felt
far more alarming. Here he was alone, with no threat from
the watchful eyes of others. No one to see the new
distinction between him and the rest, and yet here he could
not stay. He felt the sharp nauseating sensation of dread
begin to take over. In an attempt to stay calm, he focused

on his breathing, trying to control the rhythm whilst hurriedly preparing himself for the day.

He warily stepped onto the hallway tiles, and once again the glowing path directed him to work.

"Morning, sleepyhead." An excited familiar voice caught his attention.

"Morning," he drearily responded, avoiding eye contact his gleeful friend.

Noticing his less than energetic response, Corie jabbed his shoulder, forcing him to smirk in response.

Sarcastically she piped up "Wow, you're in high spirits this morning! Well even your gloominess isn't going to dampen my mood today. I have big news for you".

"Okay, tell me quick, you have about 20 seconds until I'm at my desk"

"You're ruining my build up", Corie interjected, a little deflated by his impatience.

"So, you know I've never liked myself in white, what would you say if I told you I'll soon be wearing blue?"

"Huh" Jay responded, bewildered by her meandering story.

"Oh for Christ's sake Jay, where is your head today? They're making me a guard. Soon I will be giving *you* orders" she sniggered.

He laughed, "I'm both happy for you and concerned!" he responded. Saying their goodbyes quickly, Jay walked through the sliding door to begin his work.

Without any acknowledgment of his co-workers, he seated himself at a different station today. His usual co-workers were so different to Corie, no smiles, blank faces with no expression, rarely any conversation, just work. Even though they all looked so similar; fair-haired and the same pale blue eyes, there was something unique about her. She was a rarity, he was well aware of that by now, and it made his affection for her even greater. It wasn't uncommon for her to have such an effect on him, her clear warmth and general cheery demeanour often left him feeling upbeat.

But today, it seemed as though no time with her could be enough to pull him completely free from the fear that crept over him. Within only a few minutes of entering that room, the residual anxiety surfaced. He tried to focus on his work, and methodically executed one complex task after another, stopping only to take the required doses handed to him throughout the day. The waves of emotion began to settle with each supplement he took, and although he never regained his usual sense of calm, his mood felt considerably improved. At the days end, he marched back to his quarters and turned in for the night. Shutting his eyes, he tried to relax on his bed and slowly felt himself drift off…

~

The sky opened up to me as I glided through the blue. Dusky pink clouds drifted lazily past as I weaved expertly through the air, watching the sun sink slowly, casting shadows on the ground. I spiralled downwards, scanning the earth below for my next meal. Distracted by something in the distance, I changed direction to take a closer look. Hovering in mid-air, I fixedly stared at the large crowd below, and drifted lower trying to get a closer look. Then I saw it, rows upon rows of people, all standing still, as if they were one entity, like a nest of paralysed ants. I glided over, and one by one, they turned to look at me, faces blank and expressionless. Silence filled the air; there were no voices, no laughter or any expression at all. But I heard their calls, pleading with me to save them.

~

Opening his eyes, he stared at the already brightly lit ceiling and turned to read the digits on his watch; he had 18 minutes to get ready. He must have slept through his alarm again. Standing up, he rushed to the bathroom ready to collect his morning dose; he certainly needed the boost this morning. CLANG! He jumped and twisted suddenly to face the direction of the noise, his eye catching the watch that had toppled onto the floor, sliding smoothly towards his feet. Relieved no damage was done, he crouched down and picked up the device, bringing the watch face to his own. A flash of gold caught his eye, startling him. Drawing his face towards the smooth surface of his watch, he stared wide-eyed. Without thought, he released his grip, letting the watch slam one more against the floor. It was happening again. He lurched towards the mirrored door, and paused to catch his breath, fearful of what would be staring back. His heart ricocheted against his ribcage, BA-DUMP, BA-DUMP, BA-DUMP.

He looked. The flecks of yellow had extended across the iris; large fragments of gold now encased his eye. His eyes stung as tears rushed down his face. He continued to stare at his reflection in disbelief. His eyes were blue, like all the rest, perfectly pale blue, the same blue that he saw day in and day out. Not an imperfection to be seen, so why was he staring into his own fragmented yellowing eyes instead? His mind spiralled, desperately searching for answers. *What's wrong with me*, he thought. Something must have been gravely wrong, he had never seen or heard of anyone changing like this, he knew that there was nowhere to turn. Difference would never be accepted here. His body convoluted, sobbing cries leaving his mouth. He bound his hands to his face, stifling the sounds emanating from his throat.

Standing upright, he reached for the vial that patiently waited to be consumed. He clung tightly, as the glass slid through his fingers, lubricated by his tears. He slowly sipped away, trying to calm the intermittent nauseating waves. His thoughts, which previously felt like an overflowing storm, were now beginning to subdue. Avoiding his reflection, he darted across the space, frantically grabbing at his possessions in a futile attempt to arrive on time. He felt more in control, less overwhelmed by his emotion, less scared by the changes occurring within. Stepping out of his room, he joined the sea of workers, all casually making their way to their destination. He looked at his wrist to survey the damage, knowing that his lateness would not be tolerated. His bare wrist provided no reassurance. He saw them ahead, three blue clad guards across the entrance to his office. He hesitated, considering his options, but deep down knowing there was only one. And then he saw her, despite the cloaking of her uniform, he knew it was her. He watched the third guard, tapping out a familiar rhythm on the glossy floor and without missing a beat his foot tapped back in reply. It was their song, playing on the transport the day that they arrived, an upbeat jingle that seemed so fitting for her. They sat only a row apart on the coach that day, at first not noticing one another existed. But that soon changed when the song gently echoed through the coach; Jay and Corie, two perfect strangers, moved their feet in unison to the melody.

Nervously he made his move, quietly stepping towards the guards. They watched his approach, waiting for the excuses to unfold.

'The head guard has been notified of your absence', the first male guard growled.

'I have a good reason-'

'There are no reasons or excuses that will justify your conduct' the second, taller guard interrupted.

They were right.

'Actually, this one's on me,' Corie butted in. The two guards sternly starred in Corie's direction.

'I gave worker 478 permission to visit the hospital wing early this morning. He's been complaining of stomach pain, did I forget to mention it to you?' Corie tried her best to sound convincing.

'Yes, as a matter of fact you did, we will review the correct procedures later. For now 478 you are free to return to your workstation, we will review your medical assessment later today'.

He sank into the curved steel blue chair at his desk. His nervous energy lingered knowing he had narrowly escaped punishment. But he knew that his troubles were far from over, he knew they would be looking for that medical report, how could he stop the inevitable?

The door slid swiftly open with a faint hiss. Looking up, he saw the familiar uniform, and watched as the guard surveyed the workers, wandering through the regimented rows of desks. He listened as the footsteps reached his aisle, and he cowered, lowering his head to appear absorbed in his work. The footsteps came to an abrupt halt next to him, and he watched as a crumpled piece of paper was discreetly placed on his desk. He carefully unfolded the paper, continuously paying attention to the surrounding workers, not wanting to be seen.

"You need to be more careful. I don't know what happened to you this morning, but I've arranged an appointment for you to see a doctor in the hospital wing at 14:30. You'll need to find a way to get out of here. I've helped you once, but they're watching me now, I won't be able to help you again. – Corie."

He tried to focus on his work, but his eyes were constantly drawn to the small digits in the top left hand corner of the panel, telling him that he was behind schedule with his tasks. Hurriedly, he began typing final figures into his log. Beep, beep, beep, he heard the recognisable alert, and sat back in his chair as the computers around the room powered down. As if one being, every worker rose simultaneously from their chairs, no one spoke. Without prompting they weaved quietly into their position in the line, ready to exit their room for their midday break, purely for the consumption of nourishment. He found his place in the queue, waiting for the doors to open and the march to the food court to begin. Wondering what the menu would hold today, he once again glanced at his wrist, expecting the reliable small watch to show him everything that he was required to do. To no avail, the watch was still remarkably absent. If he was to ever get his watch back before any guard realised it was missing, he knew that now would be the best time. As the march began, he planned his next steps. He knew that they would be passing his quarters in a few minutes; all he had to do was leave the crowd, collect his watch and get back in line before anyone noticed his absence. As they neared the doors to his quarters, he noted everyone's lack of interest in him, hunger was a sufficient distraction, and he darted into his room. He sped across to the watch that was still laying on the floor, scooped it into his shaking hands, and rushed out just in time to join the end of the small procession.

Sitting back down at his desk with his watch firmly on his wrist, he tried to focus on the tasks ahead of him. Time seemed to speed by as he rushed through his work. He looked over at the clock, which read 14:20. His eyes widened, knowing it was now or never. He wrapped his arms around his stomach, pulling himself up from his desk, loudly groaning as he doubled over as if in tremendous pain. No one looked up from their work. He shuffled towards the nearest guard.

"Excuse me," he paused, waiting for the guard's attention, "I feel very unwell, and I wanted permission to go see the doctor."

Saying nothing, the guard scanned his watch, checking his vitals.

"I see…" he trailed off, "your heart rate is considerably elevated, the doctor may need to alter your supplement dosage, you can leave your work for now, but we will expect you back to complete it with overtime".

"Thank you" he stepped away, and walked speedily out of the room.

After travelling the short distance to the next sector, he paused to glance at the large brightly lit green sign "Medical Wing". He reached the door of the doctor's office, right on schedule. He held his watch up to the door entry key and the panel displayed his ID and appointment details, and he waited patiently for the door to open. Once inside, he was greeted by a nurse, and instructed to wait on the only available seat. He sat down on the padded bench, taking in the peculiar assortment of equipment and the various infomercial holograms dotted around the room. His number was called and he walked through the illuminated door. Without any greeting, the doctor began her assessment.

"Place your arm here," She dictated, reaching towards his watch. He stretched his arm across the table and the doctor plugged the cable into it to access his previous medical data and current stats.

"Can you describe your current symptoms?"

"I've been having stomach cramps, they have been getting worse all day." He fidgeted in his seat, uncomfortable by the doctor's silence while noting his symptoms down.

"I see," she stared earnestly into his eyes, "are these your only symptoms?"

"Yes", he hesitantly responded, hoping she would not notice anything else of concern.

"Well it's likely to not be anything too serious. I will prescribe to you 200mg of Ritonaladine, to be taken twice daily, which should help to relieve these symptoms. You can rest for the remainder of the day." She paused, waiting for him to say something, wondering why he did not look directly at her. "Is there anything else you would like to discuss?"

"No, that's all. Thank you for your time." He stood up and stepped towards the door.

"Before you leave, I noticed on your data that your sleep pattern has been quite erratic over the past few days, and your blood pressure has been significantly higher. Do you have any explanation for this?"

He froze, clearing his throat to bide himself some time to think of a response. "The stomach pain is worse at night, it's been going on for a few days now, I'm sure your prescription will help".

The doctor nodded her head slowly, seemingly content with his response and gestured for him to leave the room. Consciously, he walked a little stooped as he passed the guard on his way back to his room. As soon as his bedroom door closed behind him he exhaled a sigh of relief and collapsed onto his bed in total exhaustion.

~

I heard a muffled sound coming from the crowd, a sound of distress. Risking a dive into the nest, I swooped down, letting the warm air carry me to the figure below. An aged man hunched over, tears rolled down his cheeks as he cried out in pain. Fleeing quickly, I moved above the next row and surveyed the figures below me. I was drawn to another sound, a shrill tormented scream escaping the mouth of the emaciated man. Without reason I flew down towards him, wanting to ease his pain, but his hands came towards me in a flurry of angry attacks. His hand sharply met my wing, sending me spiralling towards the ground. I stretched out my claws in an attempt to steady myself as I met the ground, and then I saw her. The young woman knelt on the grass, her hands stretched out beside her steadying her hunched frame. I remained still, trying to go unnoticed, feeling very aware of my vulnerability at being so close to her. Frozen to the ground, I stared at her, waiting for my opportunity to flee. Her head hung low, as if too heavy for her shoulders. I continued to watch her intently, but she did not move, it was as though she was chained to the ground. Cautiously, I stepped backwards, edging away from her reach. The grass crunched beneath my feet, but I continued, carefully watching her for any sudden movement. Without warning, she slowly raised her head in my direction, clearly drawn to the noise. Dark cavernous recesses examine me threateningly. Terrified, I took large strides to distance myself from the eyeless monster before me. Her empty sockets. Absent of all feeling, etched in my memory.

~

He opened his eyes, and felt the immediate sense of dread and panic crash down on him. He gazed fixedly at the familiar looking glass mirror as he tottered towards the sink once more. He knew it was likely that nothing good would come from this, but he found it impossible to avert his eyes from the smooth cold surface of the mirror. Wiping his eyes, which had suddenly welled up with tears, he focused on his reflection, but to his horror, the man he recognised was no longer there. He felt the cool sink edges in his tight grasp, and yet the mirror revealed the wrinkled sharp black claws clinging to the basin. His pale porcelain skin, which he usually took little notice of, was hidden beneath a swarm

21

of golden brown feathers, which fanned out as he shuddered, an ice-cold feeling rushed through him, as though his blood was drained from his veins. He stared into the bright golden yellow eyes that bore into him with a fierce intensity. He stared at the eagle and the eagle stared back.

Tears spilled down his face as he sunk down onto the unforgiving cold floor, he felt his body convulse with rasping sobs but the room was filled with an ear-piercing screech. He watched the eagle sink to the ground simultaneously, flapping its wings in distress. Despite the usual regimented timetabled life he led, in this exact moment he had absolutely no idea what to do with himself. The only thing he felt sure of was his desire to hide, to not be seen by anyone, if they did not tolerate a button out of place on a uniform, he stood no hope of a sympathetic reaction.

He scrambled around on the floor, looking for somewhere to go, somewhere that would shield him. A small space waited invitingly under his bed, barely big enough for him, but it would suffice. Sliding himself into the cramped space, he closed his eyes and waited, laying perfectly flat and still, soaking in the coldness from the floor.

It wasn't long, and he was startled from his intrusive thoughts by an overly aggressive banging at the door. Wide eyed, frozen with terror, he heard their voices.

"478 has not reported for duties this morning. We have tracked him to his quarters, it appears he has not left his room today", the gruff guard spoke into his sound piece, alerting his superiors to the situation.

"I am aware from recent interactions with 478 that he has been unwell, maybe he has worsened," Corie updated the group of guards, as they stood poised at 478's door.

Another chilling knock resonated through the room.

"478, are you there? You have been absent from your work duties this morning, which is unacceptable, no matter how "unwell" you may be. If you fail to respond within the next 5 seconds, we will enter your quarters and will search every inch of that room and this base until you have been located", Corie waited in trepidation for his response, she hoped he would be found unconscious on his bed, or that at the very least he was seriously unwell, there was little hope for him otherwise.

The silence lingered, no sound could be heard from his room. Following protocol she pressed her hand against the door and signalled to the accompanying guards to storm the room.

The once silent room was now filled with the sound of many heavy boots thudding across the expanse of the room, Peering out slightly from under his bed, he watched as the guards tore through the space, ripping every item from its place and tossing it to the ground where he lay motionless.

"His watch is here", the guard picked up the discarded watch, and tapped away at the screen to access 478's recent activity.

"His watch hasn't been worn since last night, and there have been no sightings of him on cameras outside of his quarters, so he must still be here".

The guards frantically resumed their search. "Search every millimetre of this room until he is found", screamed the head guard as he entered the room to lead his unit.

Terrified of what was to come, he lay, statue like, beneath that bed waiting. His fear entirely paralysed him, and even if he had thought of a better option in that moment, he would be physically incapable of acting on it. A pair of boots circled the perimeter of the bed. He stared at the same pair of boots as they stopped within only a few inches of his limp arm. He focused on the crimson smears that had been clumsily missed when the uniform was cleaned. He wondered if his own blood would soon be visible on someone's shoe, or whether a guard would take his time to wipe all evidence away.

Suddenly, the room became quiet, he surveyed the surrounding floor and could see the guards were now rooted to the spot, no one moved. Without warning, light flooded over him as the mattress was wrenched from the bed frame; he blinked, disoriented by the change in surroundings. The bed was lifted by the guards and tossed aside, and before he had any chance to react, he felt himself being dragged across the floor by his feet. He clawed at the ground in vain for something to hold on to, but his attackers clung on, pulling him more ferociously than before. He needed to bide time, they needed to understand that this was not his fault. He screeched for them to stop, but they couldn't understand what he had to say. Scrambling, he lashed out in fear, twisting and kicking against his attacker. His leg broke free, and in his frenzied kicks his foot connected with a guard's knee with a sickening crunch. He felt the guard's grip loosen and watched the guard drop to the floor with a blood-curdling scream.

His resistance was entirely futile, before he could react, a flurry of guards swarmed around him, restraining every limb. Exhausted by his attempts to escape, he stopped fighting them, his wings hung limply at his sides. Staring directly at the guard, he did not pull away, even when the hood was yanked over his head. He listened to the sound of marching, and watched the light flicker through the hood, as it faded from the harsh white light he was so familiar with to darkness which engulfed him. He closed his eyes, letting his body hang in the arms of the guards, their presence surrounded him like fog and in that moment he closed his eyes and gave in to all that was to come.

~

I distanced myself from the ground and the creatures below and glided in a figure of eight pattern through the darkening sky. In spite of my fear, I struggled to fly far away; I was somehow drawn to them, as if their fates were linked with my own. I looked below, surveying the little dots scattered across the ground. It was at that moment that I noticed that the uniformed patterns beneath had altered, no longer in their neatly organised rows, there were now pockets of emptiness. I could not stop myself from flying closer to them, I wanted to understand what was happening, and the sounds of their cries still haunted me. I gradually floated lower, their shapes were now defined and clear, and I could see the extent of the cavities. Where figures once stood, all that now remained were the memories and indents left in the grass. I looked at the remaining faces in the crowd and I searched for the three I had encountered before. They were no longer there; their distress was now just a memory and all that remained was the stone cold faced cluster.

~

Groggily, he slowly opened his eyes, trying to focus on his dimly lit surroundings. Hearing a faint whistling melody, he tried to turn his head to the direction of the music, but was unable to move, he could just make out the metal chains in the periphery of his vision. His head pounded as he watched a tall figure walk towards the suspended table on which he lay.

"So, you're awake? This wasn't supposed to happen." She muttered under her breath and frowned, taking in his barely coherent state.

"My head hurts...why does it hurt?" He whimpered, struggling against his restraints.

"I wouldn't do that if I were you." She stepped forward, examining him. "The amount of medicine I gave you should've made sure that you wouldn't be awake for this procedure, but it doesn't matter. It looks like you're barely awake as it is, and in no position to cause any trouble."

He watched as the nurse grabbed a syringe, filling it with a dark, tar-like substance. She whistled her tune as she worked. He continued to pull at his restraints, trying to free his bound limbs. He could feel himself slipping away again.

"This is your fault, you know." She smiled cruelly at him, "The only way to control the people is to control their will. You do something wrong, you get punished, no matter how small your crime may seem, the punishment must always evoke enough fear to deter others. There is only ever one ending to this story, and I'm always in the final chapter. Leaning over him, she injected the syringe into the pronounced vein on his arm.

"It'll all be over soon, you just lay there and stay still."

He felt the needle pierce his skin, sinking into his arm. The words "It'll all be over soon" echoed round his head. As he drifted into the deepest of sleeps, he dreamt of Corie

~

I checked the notes of Patient 478. He was admitted here over a year ago, due to hallucinations brought on by his Schizophrenia. He has been mainly unresponsive to most of the staff here, but he has taken a liking to me, so I have been assigned to do regular check-ups on him.

He often mutters to himself, most of it makes no sense, but he does say my name quite a bit. I guess I should feel flattered that he likes me enough to mention me, but most of the time it makes me feel really uncomfortable. When he is having a particularly chatty day talking about me, I keep my visits to him short!

Pushing his door open, D1T7, I walk in with my tray of supplies.

"Hi Jay, how are you feeling today? Did you sleep well? I can see you're watching your programme again, you like this one don't you?"

No response from him, as per usual. I glance towards the TV, which is showing another Attenborough documentary, this eagle episode is his favourite and often on repeat. I'm not sure how much he absorbs, he doesn't seem to react, but it seems to have a calming effect on him, so I leave it on:

"With a wingspan of up to two and a half meters, the bald eagle is one of the most formidable birds of prey. The bright yellow eagle eye is among the sharpest in the animal kingdom, with an eyesight estimated at 8 to 10 times stronger than that of the average human…"

Fixated on the screen, he watches the large eagle flying, before continuing his muttering once more.

"My eyes are yellow… Why are my eyes yellow? I'm scared… Where's… where's Corie gone?" He stuttered.

"I'm right here Jay, no need to get upset. Shall I sit with

you for a while?" I sit in the chair at his bedside, my eyes meet his, but his expression is vacant and he says nothing to me. After a few minutes of silence, I stand up and circle round his bed, my rubber shoes squeak incessantly on the glossy tiled floor. My watch beeps, time for his medication. I remove the empty IV bag, we try to keep him well hydrated and this is our only way of getting anything into him. I pick up the fresh IV bag and I notice him watching my movements as I hang the purple liquid onto the stand and hook it up to his cannula. I watch the drip, drip, drip of the Ritonaladine medication feeding through his IV, and begin to check his vitals: all seems fine today. As I listen to his pulse I am drawn to the framed pictures dotted around the ward, all animal and nature themed. Some of them are pleasant, I guess, but I genuinely detest the picture of the ants. Anytime I look in their direction, and see the thousands of ants crawling all over their nest, it makes my skin itch all over. My checks are almost complete when Jay begins his usual rant.

"Take it off. Take them off. I don't like the feathers Corie",

"I'll see you a bit later Jay, okay? You try to have a little rest". I back away from his bed, picking up my belongings as I head towards the door. I look back to check I haven't left anything behind and I watch him from a distance. I can see his lips continuing to move but I don't hang around to listen. He doesn't like it when I leave.

The End

UP IN THE AIR

By Lucy Leaver

When a little baby boy was found in a carved wooden basket, no one quite knew where he had come from. The basket itself was stunning. It appeared to be lovingly handmade and the craftsmanship was so precise it seemed almost impossible that a person could've sculpted it. The boy was also beautiful, with striking blue eyes. A couple from the local village took the little boy in and loved him like one of their own. But he wasn't like one of their own. He was always a little different from the other village children. They could see it too, and the couple watched as he became distant from everyone around him. They watched as their community turned against him. They watched as their little boy became an outcast. And an outcast he stayed.

***

All hot air balloons have to come down to Earth eventually. They can fly so high and travel so far, yet they can never stay in the air forever. Pan knew this very well. He always loved to spend his time in the air, away from the society who rejected him. He always felt free when he was beyond the clouds and away from the judging faces. The sun always shone above the clouds, and he could feel his troubles float away on the cooling breeze. With the wind transforming his jacket into a billowing work of art, Pan felt at home. The thing Pan hated about his trips was returning to the ground. The sun that had shone so brightly above the clouds seemed to deaden the closer he got to landing. Sighing, he watched as the hot air balloon touched down into the field. Back to the same old dull world. The wind that was refreshing in the sky was biting on the ground, making him shiver. Clambering out, he tied the balloon up, before wandering over the cobblestone path that led to the town. Immediately came the glares, the strange looks. The never ending muttering and whispering. Exasperated, Pan travelled along the trail that led back to the cottage he had always called home. He never understood why everyone in the village hated him so much. After all, he was a little strange, but he was still a villager like everyone else; born in the same little corner of the world.

"Pan! Hurry up, we need to go," Pan's Mother called from the kitchen. "It's the village gathering in 5 minutes and we'll be late,"

"Mother, I don't even want to go. Just leave me here, I'll be fine. No one wants me there anyway," he shouted back.

"Pan, you need to socialize more. Sometimes I worry about you spending all that time in your hot air balloon. Get in here right now,"

Pan knew he had to oblige, so he unwillingly trudged into the kitchen.

"My little boy looking so smart," Pan's Mother said lovingly as she dusted down his shirt. "You'll certainly impress all the ladies at the gathering!" she laughed.

"Can't I just go back to my hot air balloon? No one will even notice that I'm gone!"

"But Pan! You're in it all the time! You need to spend some time with your family and friends," said Mother.

"I don't have any friends, everyone hates me!" Pan exclaimed, tears streaming from his eyes

"Pan, you know that's not-"

"It is true! I've never been accepted and you know it. I'm leaving! I'm going right now and you can't stop me!"

29

He stormed out the door and ran all the way to the meadow, his feet flying over stones and leaves, his face bright red and hot with anger. His heart was pounding inside his chest, and he felt sick. He knew what he needed to do, where he needed to go: The hot air balloon. Pan raced over and fumbled with all the knots keeping it tied down and safe. No one could keep him tied down now… they'd done it for eighteen long years already. He pulled out the matches and lit the flame, which would fuel his escape into the air.

Pan laughed and wiped his eyes as the hot air balloon rose into the air, flying up and up as he floated away from all his problems. Up in the sky, no one could judge him, or treat him like something he wasn't. He could imagine that he was the only person in the world. He was free.

But deep down he knew he wasn't. The hunger to be accepted still persisted within him, gnawing at his insides with a tireless drive. Even when he was up in the air, he still couldn't fill that hole. Something was missing. He had tried so many times to fit in, but no matter how hard he struggled, it never worked. As much as he tried to pretend otherwise, all he really wanted was to be normal.

Pan swallowed and pushed that feeling away. He watched as he and the balloon emerged over the delicate clouds, marvelling at the beauty. His eyes widened as he surfaced, and the sun became visible again. It was always sunnier above the clouds, no matter the weather. It could be the rainiest day, and yet he could still escape reality into a world of sunshine and acceptance. He lent over the edge, greedily absorbing his surroundings. There was the sun he knew and loved! There was the breeze that allowed him to fly far and wide, as if he were nothing but a feather! Drunk on relief he walked across the hot air balloon, oblivious to anything but himself. Without warning, he tripped on a rope, sending him toppling over the edge. He screamed as he watched the hot air balloon disappear above him. He fell and fell, through the clouds and back down to the world where the sun never shined as bright.

He waited for the sickening crack as he hit the ground, bracing himself with eyes shut tight as possible. But it never came. He seemed to be hovering slightly above the ground, held up by some incredible force. Nervously he opened his eyes. What in the world could be stopping him from reaching the ground? To his surprise, people surrounded him. He waited for the glares, the strange looks. The never ending muttering and whispering. However, something even stranger had happened; the townspeople had helped him. They lowered him to the ground, slowly and carefully, and Pan flusteredly untangled himself from the net that had broken his fall.

Alarmed, Pan brushed himself off and stood up. He turned round and completed a full circle. They were all just like him. The same face, the same clothes. The same home.

'Welcome home Pan.' Pan's Mother said as she emerged from the crowd.

And just like that, Pan was set free. It all finally made sense. He belonged somewhere. He always had, but he'd never seen it before. He wasn't strange or odd… just different.

And he was no longer alone.

AVERAGE

By Amber Burgess

Isn't it funny how there are never any stories that just follow the life of someone random?

Just an 'average Joe' who's doing nothing much, and then accidentally just happens to save the world or break free from whatever is holding them down? It's always someone special - someone particularly brave, clever or strong. I guess that's just how these stories tend to work, but does it have to be like that?

I'm really not very brave, clever, or strong at all. Nothing has led up to me deciding to do what I'm about to do; in fact, I didn't decide at all. Other people just decided for me, without letting me have any choice in the matter. The same as always.

You see, I was chosen for what's about to happen for the very reason that I'm boring and not very different from anyone in any way. I'm ordinary, meaning I'm unsuspicious, making me perfect for the job.

I'm not terrible at what I do, but I'm not remarkably good either. I'm average.

***

I wake with a start as the morning bell rings at 5am. I never get used to it, no matter how many times I hear it. Yawning and stretching, I check my tasks for the day… Just the same old daily chores that no one ever wants to do. But of course

I have to do them, just like I have to stay here. I don't have a choice. After all, I've never had a choice. Everything I do is decided by someone else. From the minute I was taken from my home and caged up in these halls four years ago, I have never been my own person, never even had the chance.

Quickly, I get dressed into my navy blue day uniform, which has my labourer number firmly stamped just above the breast pocket in bright white ink. 6174. The Master did consider getting us all tattooed with our numbers on our necks but decided just putting it on the uniforms would be cheaper and easier.

A deep ache in the pit of my stomach arises as I remember what today is. From across the room Clementine wearily raises his eyebrows at me. I smile worriedly at him. Today is the day that Clementine and I must carry out the escape plan.

Now, ever since they captured us and brought us here, of course I wished we could escape somehow. But I never thought it would actually happen. Over the last four years, I have come to terms with the idea that this is my reality: my life. That I would and could never be anything more than a servant, an object, a bird in a birdcage, and that was fine by me.

And besides, I've always been certain that if anyone would, I wouldn't be the one to defy the Master and break free - I don't have the soul of a freedom fighter, I have the soul of a mouse.

I begin to tremble as the daunting day ahead begins to really settle in my mind. If I get caught trying to escape it'll be certain death - no, at that point death would be a luxury. So it'll be the rest of my already sorry, hopeless life made ten times more painful. I know plenty of rebels that have defied the rules like I will today. They are taken away to... no one really knows where. Rumours spread amongst us about where the rebels might go and what might happen there, but it's just gossip. All we do know is that once they come back they are changed. Physically they mostly look fine. No visible bruising or anything like that. But after someone comes back from wherever the rebels go, they only speak when they are told to by the Master or his other staff. If you try to talk to them, they just look at you as if you're speaking a different language. I suppose they are traumatized in some way to the point where they are like robots, simply obeying their commands. They behave after that.

This is why I'm so terrified about today.

It stays on my mind all morning, the knowledge that we are going to finally break free. Break free or be broken. I need to be unsuspicious, meek and timid. Just a lowly servant carrying out my tasks, that's all. I scamper up the winding marble staircase, my footsteps echoing a little too loudly for someone trying to go unnoticed. As I carry the Master's clean laundry up to his room, I tremble at the idea of conducting the first step of the plan: locate the master key. Nervously, I knock on the door.

"Clean laundry, sir...!" I wait for an answer, but to my relief no sound comes. I step into the Master's luxury suite, admiring the gigantic four-poster bed, the lavish decorations scattered around the room, the tall windows letting in beams of the morning sunlight... I shake my head at these irrelevant thoughts. I have a task to complete and I must be fast. There's no telling when the Master will return. Carefully, I sift through the draws in his desk. I can't leave any trace that I looked in here, or I'll be in for it. The plan will be ruined and I'll never see the light of day again.

Then I see it. A tiny glass box with an ornate engraving of a key on it nestled right at the back of the drawer. Perfect.

Just then, I hear thumping footsteps. He's back. I quickly grab the box and bury it in the basket with the dirty clothes.

Not even a second later, the door flings open and the Master saunters in. I jump. Just the sight of him makes me shiver.

The Master is a very tall man. He towers over everyone, looking down on you with malice in his dark, cruel eyes. He has longish brown hair that falls awkwardly by his ears. He wears an ill-fitting white suit that isn't actually that nice; if I had my own personal tailor, I would wear something a bit more creative than an ugly white suit. His face is like a rat's, and his odd little hands are always balled up into fists, as if he's constantly angry. He is. That's why even his closest friends are terrified of him, and that's how he stays in power.

"What are you doing here!?" He booms, making me flinch.

"I'm putting away the clean laundry, sir." I say, swallowing hard.

"Well, get on with it! I don't have all day!" Yes he does. He has all the time in the world to do whatever he wants. He lounges around all day, doing nothing but bossing everyone around, and no one can do anything about it.

"Yes sir." I reply meekly.

Hastily, I fumble for the basket of dirty laundry and slip through the door. I run until I reach a corner and collect my shaking mess of a body. I rummage through the laundry basket to find the glass box... Imagine if the Master were to find it out of place somewhere-

There it is.

For a few moments, I let myself breathe. That was intense. I can feel my heart pounding in my throat and I am breathing so fast it's making me dizzy.

Attempting a deep breath, I gather all my thoughts and prepare myself for the next step of our scheme to freedom: I need to give the key to Clementine so he can lock up the guards, making sure they won't prevent our escape. Then he'll come and give it back to me so I can unlock the gate and set everyone free. I walk down the spiral staircase leading to the laundry room. Dumping the Master's crumpled suits into an empty washing machine, I grab the box. In a mad panic, I sprint across the hallway. Running to the dorm to give Clementine the key. I smash the box and throw the shards of glass into a random laundry basket nearby. The key is a lot less bulky and suspicious without the box. As I hold the key in my hand, I realise how tiny it is. So strange how such a tiny object can hold so much power. Kind of like me… small but mighty.

I reach the dorm and see Clementine waiting for me.

"Here's the key. Go!" I whisper to him, handing the key over.

We nod to each other and he leaves the room. I watch as he walks down the hall. I wait a few minutes before heading over to the garden. This is where it gets really risky; none of my chores are in the garden. If I get caught, I can't bluff my way through this.

The gardens are full of luscious green trees and colourful flowerbeds. There are so many people that have to tend to the array of plants at all times. But most importantly, at the front of the main garden are the gates, our route to freedom. Now we'll see if I really am so perfect for the job.

I grab a rake lying on the ground and pretend I'm busy. I make my way across the garden, attempting to look like I'm actually on shift here. Everyone else is counting on me, so I can't mess up…

I reach the lavish main gates at the front of the palace. Immense structures, with the tiniest of details and carvings, depicting the timeline of the rise of the Master and his civilization. But I don't have time to admire pretty things, I need to free everyone.

Where is Clementine? He was meant to lock up the guards in the cellar so we could escape. He should be done by now-

Just as I start to panic, I see a figure in the distance, gasping for air. As the figure gets closer I realize it's a very flustered Clementine.

"Clementine…?"

"They- They're coming!" He puffs hurriedly. "The guards- be quick!" In the distance the mob of guards slowly inch forward. He thrusts the key at me and I frantically shove it into the lock. There is a moment of silence as we wait for the click that means the gate is unlocked.

I shove the heavy gates forward, giving me a small gap to escape through and let everyone else out.

"Where is everyone?" I hiss.

"They're supposed to be here by now! I don't know what's keeping them!" Clementine replies worriedly. I start manically pacing back and forth. The guards are coming for us and no one else is here to escape. I have failed. I turn around as the shouts of the guards reach us, accepting my doomed fate.

"Go!" Clementine yells. He shoves me through the gates and pulls them back closed behind me.

"What? I can't!"

"Go and don't look back. We'll be fine without you… It'll work out!" Clementine shouts as I hesitate, staring back at him.

"I can't just leave you!" I object.

"You have no choice!" He calls. The guards will drag him away in a matter of seconds and I'll be next if I'm not fast. I really don't have a choice now. Clementine sacrificed himself for our plan, and I can't let that go to waste. I can only hope that the Master won't be too harsh on him - oh, who am I kidding? I will probably never see Clementine again, and if I do he will only be a shadow of who he was. So I can't just give up on this now. For Clementine, I have to go.

"I'll come back for you, I swear. I can't leave you, or anyone to live and die in this place!"

"Then go, be free. Maybe we'll meet again. It's been an honour"

We solemnly nod at each other, before I quickly leave.

My mind racing just as fast as my legs, I run off the long, topiary-lined driveway. I reach the road leading to the rest of the world, to freedom.

So, it's the end of this story… but not of mine. I've been set free from the cruel Master and his palace, but my friends have been left behind. I can't betray them or myself by leaving them there forever.

So I'll return, yes; I'll return and I'll rescue them. I've got this far. And hey, that's all because I'm unremarkable, meek and timid. Average. And yet somehow I have done what has been impossible for the most remarkable of us.

OUTSIDE

By Lucas Fernee

I opened my eyes.

There was a beautiful forest in front of me, with a gateway illuminated by the summer's light. The pathway was made of dusty white slabs, lined by smaller slabs. Any cracks in the tiles were engulfed with thick green moss. It was soft and springy and looked like little trees growing through the stone. The light from the sun reflected off the creamy surface of the slabs, which were the colour of buttermilk candy: heavenly. The shade of the trees made the warmth of the pavement appealing. Shadows danced in the light, refracting hues of lush pink. But as the path went on, the less kind it seemed. The warm green leaves became menacing. The shadows stopped dancing and became a cadaverous blanket of night.

Statues of majestic golden monkeys sat on the earth beside the path. Patches of grass surrounded them in front of the dense forest. Whenever the light hit the sandy earth under them, it sparkled like a million diamonds embedded in the rock. The light started to fade in the dark but beguiling forest.

The forest itself was captivating but also had a threatening demeanour. The trees whispered to each other in the breeze, whilst the sun's light gently caressed the green clouds of leaves. The early morning dew became liquid diamonds twisting around their lustrous surface. I looked further up to the clusters of verdant leaves, and the sky peered through gaps in the trees: an ephemeral experience. The golden glow of the sun made the leaves' edges appear aqua.

The gate was a vivid red, as radiant as a ruby. The light escaping the trees' grasp made the gate ignite in a thousand burning shades. The oriental structure of the gate was remarkably enthralling and bewitching. The trees' branches loomed over the gate, casting shadows, which expelled ripples of hazy sunlight. An old rope hung from the gate, creating an appeal of ancient beauty. As I strolled through, I brushed my fingers across the wooden blocks hanging from the rope: they felt rough and worn out. The gate itself contrasted this. It was smooth and polished. There wasn't a single crack. It gave off a strong aroma of fruit, which was strange as there was no fruit in the forest.

Past the gate, the forest stretched on for as far as the eye could see. As I meandered down the path, a wind started to build and brushed against my skin. As the breeze continued to blow, the sea of leaves above me created waves that touched the sky. I kept walking. My pace began to slow and then the forest vanished. The light became overwhelming.

Then I realised. The torture was over. They had killed me.

I was free.

THE CRASH

By Tegan Fitzgerald

Friday 9th July 2021

Moonlight lit up the snow-covered land. Stars painted the sky with glowing lanterns of gold and silver. Icy country roads coiled through the fields as Matilda drove into breaking dawn. The radio chattered in the background. Outside, the occasional owl hooted. But, in the horizon, distant sirens grew louder. The road trembled as two shining eyes grew bigger through the trees. Something roared like a tiger, piercing the once tranquil and serene atmosphere. The screeching metal of the breaks were too late.

Crunch! Windows shattered. The sound of tinkling shards of glass danced down the road. Her motionless body was thrown back and forth, as the car flipped through the air. Smoke clustered the sky and fire crackled from the engines.

Visions. Blurry images of men tugging at her arms. Nothing.

Tuesday 27th July 2021

Weeks later, after the crash, she never felt the same. More visions, blackouts, and sleepless nights haunted her. Days passed. Unnerving images tangled her thoughts: her family and friends, and even people she passed in the streets; fatal images of their death, engraved in her mind. The doctors kept saying she was fine and amazingly healthy for what had happened. Yet she knew her heart was beating that little bit faster, and that her brain buzzed with more energy than ever before.

Wednesday 28th July 2021

She sat in a cosy restaurant and was greeted by an unfamiliar figure. A friendly old man sat in her presence.

"Hello!" The delicate old man's soothing voice made her curious. "What are you doing in this cafe lounging about?" He chuckled. "You are still young - unlike me. What do you want to do in your life? "

Matilda was in a daze and was unsure what to say. However, not wanting to be rude, she replied, "I want to become a primary school teacher … I want a family, I want a loving husband … I want a long life, I guess."

"I want to live another seven years to get to a hundred, and then I don't care how I move on," the man laughed, and then he gasped for air, reaching out for a tissue to cough into.

"I am sorry, that is impossible. You will die in exactly 1 year and 58 days from now, in your bed, alone, from heart failure." Matilda stared into empty space, like she was frozen in time.

"How do you know that!?" his voice started to shake. "Who are you?!" The fear in his voice awoke her from her trance, before she realised he was gone.

"Wait. No!" one question buzzed in her head: how did she know?

Breaking her chain of thoughts, the waiter came to ask if she was finished, however, she instantly knew his end. He would go on a holiday and go canoeing, but it ended the wrong way up, capsized in a river.

Her life just has a bit more confusing. However, one theory occupied her head.

Saturday 19th April 2039

As most fairy tales go, she was married to her dream husband and had four beautiful children. She lived in the perfect house with the perfect life. She promised herself never to look at how they die because she wanted to enjoy every moment with them and not wait for them to die, however, she never forgot the encounter with the old man and wondered, from time to time, if he actually died.

Years went by as she saw her family's lives unfold before her, yet they didn't see hers. She didn't age or change at all. As wrinkles cursed her partner's face, she stayed young and beautiful. Soon her own children looked older than she did.

As times go on people move on. What seemed like a dream soon turned into a nightmare.

Wednesday 09th July 2200

Soon no one but her sat in the empty house. Tears burnt her cheeks. She had no one to talk to, no friends or family. She could never enjoy having small talk with someone because all she saw was unhappiness of the future. She had already paid the price of making friends and watching them grow old as their body gave up on them, and she knew they would never understand.

Wisdom comes with age they say, so as you could imagine technology evolved. People were out of their jobs and robots eventually took over. Every car, plane and boat was electric and autonomous; vines crawled up every lamppost and hung from the roof to roof. It should have been like heaven, full of life and magical things; instead it definitely felt like hell. Every person she ever talked to, anyone who showed any affection to her was coldly rejected with the shake of her head; she did not want to feel the heavy loss of a loved one again.

Her life turned into a spiral of loneliness and she tumbled straight into it.

She had had enough. . .

Friday 18th January 2201

There she sat, on the edge, as the bitter breeze nipped her skin. The occasional vehicle zoomed past as the grey sky shifted to night. She glared beneath her dangling feet, but nothing but mist painted her fate. Her weak trembling hands clenched the thin air as she took her last breath, so she thought.

She rolled off.

SPLASH!

Saturday 19th January 2201

She awoke with a startled gasp. She should be dead; she should be in heaven or hell - she did not care at this point. As days went on, she tried - and failed – to kill herself many times: starting fires, using electricity in her bath, jumping off rooftops, and yet she always awoke in her bed, unharmed and dazed.

Friday 9th July 2212

Matilda lay down in the newest car. It was made of a composite smart-glass, so you can have it see through if you wanted or change it to look different. The seats went back into a bed and there was one button (the on button) then a screen where you type where you want to go and it takes you.

As the car slowly moved down a country road, Matilda gazed at the bleak wasteland either side of her. Mounds of rubbish blocked the view of the horizon, dumped there by the one world government. The occasional rat came skittering out with some form of rotting food in its grips while fog just sat like a permanent blanket.

She lay back, gazed out of the sunroof, and noticed the

only lights in the sky: six beautiful stars. They shone like priceless diamonds. However, something about the appearance of them made her feel at peace. As a radio chatted in the background, all of a sudden, the mounds of litter started to crumble like a sand.

The sound of an engine rumbled louder than ever as a car swerved into sight and at high speed. This car was not right. This car wasn't like the cars now; it was an older one, with gears and petrol. It had a scratched metal bonnet and dents, like it was just in a crash.

She glared at the stars one last time before shutting her eyes.

The screeching of metal pierced the atmosphere as breaks were slammed. CRASH! Windows shattered. The sound of tinkling shards of glass danced down the road. Her motionless body was thrown back and forth. The car flipped through the air, as smoke clustered the sky.

It ended how it started, but this time she wasn't scared. She was happy. She will finally be reunited with her family.

A new star was placed in the sky that night.

BROKEN SILENCE

By Jessica Harris

The compound was silent.

I could hear my breath echoing off the metallic walls. I tiptoed through the halls as quietly as I could, yet I still sounded like an ogre compared to the air surrounding me. I edged closer to the bright light and my breath caught in my throat as the anticipation became unbearable.

I stopped. Behind the door were the muffled clash and bang of pots and saucepans, and the grunts of frustrated creatures. The temptation to turn around and run back to the safety of my dorm was high, yet I knew I had to do this. Gently, I pressed my palms against the door and pushed it slightly, trying to avoid the creak that I knew would arise from any sudden movement. The clanging continued until… it didn't. The banging stopped. I could hear the loud breathing of the monsters as I snuck into the kitchen.

There were two large, ferocious creatures standing around the table. Metal pans dropped to the ground as they stood in painful silence. I froze. It took me a moment to realise that they were looking at me. They had their fronts facing the table, but their heads were turned to look at me. No one should be able to turn their heads like that. I stood in this quiet place. My hands shook from gripping the door handle. I had two options. Either I could turn back and run, ruining all the progress I had made, or I could move forward, refusing to break eye contact. I chose the second option: never would I back down from a challenge.

My eyes felt as though they were going to crack from dryness as I edged my way around the creatures. It was a brutal staring contest, except if I blinked, I would probably die.

As I edged my way to the other side of the room, the creatures never broke eye contact with me. I felt behind me for the exit, the door handle singeing my hands as the warmth of my flesh hit the cold metal.

I've gotta go. I've gotta go. If I don't escape, I'll be kept here forever. They'll hold me here forever.

The doors clashed as I slammed all of my body weight against them. The chain that hung around the outside handles clanged against the cold metal. One more smash into the door and it burst open.

Sunlight flooded my view as I threw my arm in front of my face. It took a while for my eyes to adjust but when they did, I could see the beauty of the world around me. The world I had been deprived of my entire adult life.

As I inhaled the fresh summer air, my mind went back to reality. Erupting behind me, and cutting through the peaceful sound of birds, were bellowing alarms and angry shouting as armed men charged the compound. I laughed and ran, ran as fast as I could.

The concrete came into view as I passed the main gate. The rusted sign stood as tall as ever:

'Pentonville Sanitarium For The Criminally Insane'.

ORBITAL

By Harry West

"Come on Robinson, get out of your sleeping pod and come get your rations!" yelled the guard.

Hugh opened his eyes and looked at his grey, lifeless room. It was quite unremarkable, with nothing of note apart from his exercise equipment and the window that let him look at the great blue marble the prison was orbiting. He opened his sleeping pod and hovered out into the middle of his cell.

Hugh oriented himself in his grey cube and pushed himself towards the door. The hatch on his door opened and he was greeted by the steely grey eyes of Officer Franklin.

"Rations for the week," he said, as he put the packets of food through the food hatch and then proceeded to slam both of them shut.

"Thanks," Hugh mumbled. The clicking of the guard's magnetic boots echoed throughout the hallways of the prison as he walked away. Hugh gently floated to his cell wall and carved another tally onto it, sighing, "Day 3650."

Hugh spent most of his time staring out of his window. It was one of the few things he could do apart from exercise and reading, but these had started to feel like a chore. It was incredibly lonely in the cell: he had no pictures of his family, and the only thing reminding him of home was the view of Earth.

In normal prisons you would see other prisoners, but

not here, not in this place. Although Hugh was not sure he would want to see the other inmates as he had heard via the guards' conversations that many people were in here for terrorism, murder and other crimes that Hugh didn't want to think about. He opened his rations and started eating breakfast, staring down at the world he missed so very much.

THWACK. Hugh threw a crisp right hand hitting the guy directly in the eye. Adrenaline began to pump through his veins; the music seemed to get louder. The guy came back at him throwing a wild haymaker. BANG.

Hugh hit the side of his cell.

How long had he been out for? He must have fallen asleep after eating breakfast and drifted into the wall. Sleeping without a sleeping pod keeping you anchored to one place was incredibly dangerous. He was glad to be awake now and away from the nightmare he was having. He was also incredibly lucky that he wasn't seriously hurt - he could have drifted into the exercise equipment and hit his head - especially in the frail state he was in.

Hugh was supposed to do the same routine every day for 2 ½ hours to avoid muscular atrophy, a nasty side effect of his current situation. He had not done his exercise for six months and had begun to lose muscle and bone mass as his body adapted to the weightless environment of space. This isn't such a big problem when you're in space but when you are released and go back to Earth, it is a big problem, a big problem indeed. Your body will get crushed by Earth's gravity and your heart won't be strong enough to pump blood around it. This is a serious issue for the prison as it's their duty to make sure that you get back to Earth in a healthy state.

Hugh's terms were simple: let him see his family and he would stop the strike.

~

It was a crisp autumn morning. Natalie sat on the porch staring out into the woods that were at the rear of the house. In a few minutes she would be seeing a man she hadn't seen in ten years, a man she feared would be different from when she last saw him. Natalie looked at the picture of her husband that she had kept with her all this time. It showed a young, clean-shaven, well-built man with tight cut black hair and an olive complexion. He had joy-filled brown eyes that would brighten Natalie's day whenever she looked into them. She headed back into the house where her son, daughter and in-laws were.

"It's almost time now, guys," Natalie said. "Let's turn on the TV and connect to the video call."

They sat on the sofa, all bunched up together, and her son Russell flicked on the TV to enter the call. They were met by a slender man with glasses who looked at them.

"Hello Robinsons, I will be connecting you to the video call from the Duffield Orbital Prison shortly. For safety reasons this meeting will be recorded."

The screen then went static and they were met by another man. He wore a grey jumpsuit, had black unkempt hair and was sporting a beard covering most of his lower face. He was middle aged and had small wrinkles beginning to form on the olive skin that covered his frail body. His eyes were brown and looked like all the joy had been taken from them. Tears began to form in his eyes, which he wiped away promptly, the droplets drifting away.

"Long time no see," he said with a smile.

~

For this meeting, Hugh had been given a small tablet which he would have to give back later. He pressed the on button and waited for the operator to connect him to the call. The screen was black for a few minutes but then he was finally connected. He greeted them and smiled. For the first time in 10 years he was finally seeing his family. His wife, Natalie, was as beautiful as the day he had left. She smiled and he could see tears in her eyes. He looked at his kids who he barely recognised. Russell looked so much like him; he was 15 now. Hugh's daughter looked very different as well. She was three when he left and had grown so much.

"It's great to see you son," Hugh's father said. Both his parents had gone grey and looked much older then he remembered.

"It's incredible to see you all," he said, fighting the urge to break down into a crying mess.

This was the greatest moment of Hugh's life. He was reunited with his family, even if it was only through a screen. They all conversed for ten minutes until Natalie asked for some alone time with Hugh and the others obliged.

"Hugh, I think we are almost there with the case we are building on the Duffields," she said.

"Please, Natalie, can we not talk about this now? They could be watching this call," he replied in a firm tone.

"Yes, I understand that, but this is important for you to kno........."

The screen went black.

"Natalie?" Hugh asked. "Nat?" he asked again. He repeated her name again and again, with more desperation filling his voice. He threw the tablet at the wall, but it just floated in place. He began to yell and scream. "You bastards! Why would you do this? My family! My family!"

Six months of deteriorating his muscles for only ten minutes with his family. The feeling of defeat engulfed his mind. He curled up and sobbed, floating into the centre of the room.

After the guards retrieved the tablet, Hugh curled up by the window and watched the world spin beneath him. He then thought about that fateful night, the night where his life changed.

It had been the 30th birthday party of one of Natalie's friends from the law firm she worked at. Towards the end of the party when Natalie and Hugh began to leave, they heard a man say something to Natalie to the side of them.

"Hey beautiful, wanna hang out with us?"

Hugh turned around to see who this guy was and find out why he had the gall to catcall his, then, fiancée. He was a man who looked about Hugh's height but seemed a bit younger.

"Don't speak to me like that," Natalie replied.

"Or what?" he said with a snarl.

"Just don't speak to her like that," Hugh said, jumping into the conversation.

"What're you gonna do, big man?" He then squared up to Hugh, grinning in his face. Hugh began to step back when the guy swung at him, only slightly missing Hugh's chin.

THWACK. Hugh threw a crisp right hand hitting the guy directly in the eye. Adrenaline began to pump through his veins; the music seemed to get louder. The guy came back at him throwing a wild haymaker. It missed.

Hugh responded with another huge right hand, knocking the guy out. He soon came to realise that this was the worst mistake of his life.

The sleazy man he had knocked out was Xavier Duffield, son of the billionaire Ulysses Duffield, who also happened to be the main financier of the prison. As a result of the scuffle at the party, Mr Duffield had pulled some strings to get Hugh sent to the Orbital Prison. Mr Duffield was the definition of a sociopath. Hugh had seen many interviews of him on TV: he was all smiles and laughs, but you could see that behind his eyes there was actually nothing there, just an entity pretending to be human. His huge wealth allowed him to get the best legal officials. They made Hugh seem like a violent offender worthy of being sentenced to a lifetime in isolation.

~

Natalie anxiously waited outside of the office. Ten years. Ten years she had been building this case, carefully crafting every word in the file she held in her shaking hands. The door in front of her opened and a middle aged woman came peering out.

"Natalie Robinson?" she said, looking at Natalie through her wire rimmed glasses. "Mr Duffield will see you now."

Natalie stood up and all the anxiety faded from her being; she was ready to do what she had wanted to do for an entire decade. She entered the room. It was as cold and unfeeling as the man sitting inside of it. No colour and no decorations, apart from one abstract painting, which too was colourless.

"Hello, Mr Duffield," she said, trying to keep her composure.

"Hello, Mrs Robinson," he responded with a fake smile. "To what do I owe the pleasure of this visit?"

Without a word she slammed down the file she had in her now still hands. He opened the file and his smile immediately disappeared, replaced by an emotionless flat expression.

"Here are all the bribes and everything illegal you did during Hugh's trial," She said with a sense of triumph in her voice. "I thought you may like to see it. I would be expecting a call from the authorities anytime now."

"Get out," he said, his stony face expression not wavering for a second. Natalie grinned: she knew she had won.

~

"Come on Robinson, get out of your sleeping pod," yelled the guard. It had been a week since Hugh had spoken with his family. He opened his groggy eyes, looking out of his window. "Hurry up Robinson, I've got something to tell you."

This pricked Hugh's attention. He unzipped the sleeping

bag and manoeuvred his way over to the door, expecting the eye hatch to open. However, this time it didn't. Instead, the door opened and he was met by the steely grey eyes of Officer Franklin.

This was weird. That door was not opened very often. *An inspection maybe,* thought Hugh.

"I've got some good news," he said. "Your case has been overturned. We have arranged for your transportation home and it will arrive shortly."

"What?" Hugh asked, confused. "I am sorry, what did you say?" He began to feel faint.

"You're innocent," the officer replied. "I'm going to leave and let you process this," he said, closing the door.

Hugh floated to his window still in shock. He stared out into space, looking at Earth. His vision began to blur and he sobbed with happiness. Nat had done it! He was going home! After all these years, after all this lost time, he was going back to his family. Hugh composed himself and looked back out to the blue marble that floated in the ink black void of space.

Finally, freedom.

STARS

By Aisha Quddus

It's boring, viewing the aging stars through the same window, in the same area, in the same room. My room. There is nothing wrong with my room, however; I like it very much. I merely wish to observe the ravishing stars up close.

My withered body limits my desires. My stiff legs are wheelbound due to arrogance, my chair occasionally operated by my levering arms but usually steered by a younger lady whose name I can't remember, not that it really matters. My deteriorating vision, barely functional, has blurred, although I can still glimpse the unreachable stars. My overwhelmed mind may wander off sporadically, but my childhood love for gazing into glittered space remains fixed.

I'm babied within a peaceful care home, except I hate it. There is nothing wrong with the elderly home either, but they're the reason I can't live my childhood dream: I'm not allowed on the main balcony, the only place I could ever view the enchanting stars perfectly.

Outrageous.

They said I'm too fragile. It could be dangerous or something. I forgot the real reason but does that matter? No, no it doesn't. I want something and I'm going to get it. Rules are rules but dreams are dreams. I've been treated like a kid for years but can't truly live like one. I've waited long enough. My patience has faded.

I'm ready.

I approach the wooden door. The muffled creak of the ungreased hinges echoes momentarily. Then I see it, the end of the corridor: the destination. The balcony. I run my fingers through the creases of the cold plastic bound upon the wheels once more, before eagerly jolting myself forward with a push. The wheels glide across the stone-cold tiling making a slight whistling sound. The breeze strokes my face. I get closer, and closer, and closer until I reach the balcony door. My hands are shaking as I grab the handle. Then I open it and slowly slide out.

And it's beautiful.

An endless stream of sparkling glitter in deep space.

THAWED

By Isabelle Clarke

Cold, Glacial, Polar; the first thoughts that came to my mind when I woke up again. I sat, for some reason dripping wet, on stinking mould and in complete darkness. I tried to remember why I was there. I sat for what could have been hours before I decided to stand up and investigate. I pushed myself onto my feet, and as my back straightened the last couple of inches, a tidal wave of memories came crashing over me, throwing me back to the ground. The doorbell, the cold outside, the grip of his rough hands against my arm, but most importantly the sickly sweet smell of the gag, laced with something unspeakable.

No signs of life had presented themselves to me in a while, so I decided to search for a light source. It must have been around half past eleven when I was taken; I remember glancing at my watch before bed. The icy metal clamping my wrist told me I hadn't taken it off. After listening to my own footsteps echoing off walls for a long time, I found a passageway illuminated by an almost godly light. It emanated from the open door like a picture from a holy book, representing my freedom from this frozen prison I had been held in. I set off towards it, a spring in my step, a spring of hope.

As soon as I was close enough to the light, I glanced at my watch. But the hands had come to a halt, cold and lifeless as if they were dead. I had no clue of the time; my only indicator was the blinding sunshine outside. Taking a deep breath, I took a step towards the door. And another. And another. Before I knew it, I was at the exit, looking through. It took a long time for my eyes to adjust, so when my hand first met the cold wood of the doorframe, all I could see was white, piercing my eyes. When the edges of my vision became clearer, I paused for a moment, and stepped into the world outside.

~

My feet met hard, glossy marble streets. They were empty - or so I thought. I looked down to see tiny creatures, almost octopus-like, gliding across the floor. Long bodies rested on a slug-like foot, with tiny shoulders and a long neck. Large eyes were set into a bald, seed-shaped head. They didn't look at my face; they must have only seen my feet, ginormous compared to them, and yet they didn't seem confused. Did this happen to them often? These otherworldly critters and my destroyed watch made me concerned about the time. Not just what hour, but on a larger scale, like years or perhaps even decades. What was happening? Thoughts struck my brain like arrowheads. I did not know what these diminutive creatures were, but I didn't want to just stand here and wait for something to happen. I thought it was worth a shot to try to communicate.

"What year is it?"

A small creature stopped and cocked its head up at me. I tried one more time.

"What year is it?"

The creature didn't move, so I gave up and turned around to explore more.

"2421" it mumbled in a croaky voice.

I whipped around, but the creature had gone, melted back into the crowd. 2421. The fact shook me to my very core. What happened over those years? I needed to find out what had gone on in the world during my coma-like nap.

~

I asked myself questions as I walked. Where was I walking to? How could I find out how I got here? Are these tiny creatures the humans of the future? It took me a long time to gather my thoughts, but when I did, I decided to go back to the place it all started. The warehouse.

When I made it back there, I traced long, winding pathways until I found myself in the dark, musty room where I woke up. I spotted a thin stream of light coming from a window, and I just managed to open it. What I saw next made me gasp. Rows upon rows of metal containers, some filled with water, and some filled with humans, from my time, frozen in ice. Green, cloudy ice, churning concoctions of chemicals, which kept the ice frozen for hundreds of years. Though I was still confused, two of my questions had been answered; how I got here, and one which had been recently added: why I was soaked? I had clearly been frozen in this ice, as had many others. But the thing that struck me most, as I stood staring at the desolate land of frozen bodies, was whether anyone else survived. I left the building of horrors, and took off in search of something, anything that would lead me to a source of information about my confusing past.

I found what must have been a shop, full of cabinets showing various items, each with a tiny button in front of it. Not being one of these creatures, I couldn't fit inside the shop myself, so I stuck a finger in, and pressed a button. *'Declined'* it read in a tiny print. *'No money left on hand'.* These must have been scanners which read your fingerprints, like tiny card machines. I retrieved my finger and decided to continue exploring.

I wandered around town, much further than I had before, finding things like tiny libraries with the same buttons, and a tiny cinema with individual booths for every person, and family booths. Everywhere I went I had to be careful n0t to step on these tiny beings, which was incredibly difficult as they were everywhere. How much overpopulation occurred, I thought to myself as I narrowly avoided collision with a building. Then I saw him.

I nearly passed out the first time I saw him. Another human from my age. I walked towards him.

"Dylan Morgan" he spoke as he offered his hand.

"Ariah Thompson," I said, as I took it, and shook it firmly.

"Come with me. I have a lot to show you."

PROVEN

By Alice Monk

The metal clang of the door echoed through the room and ricocheted through my ears as the guard slammed it shut. My shaky legs collapsed beneath me as I slid down the cold, rough wall. Closing my eyes tight, I did not want to be faced with the plain white wall, which I would see every day for the foreseeable future. No, rephrase that. The rest of my life. But why? Why me? Why was I chosen to take the blame for his doing? His crime. His mistake.

A small tear slowly fell down my face before they started flowing down my face like waterfalls and my breathing hitched. I started viciously wiping them away but soon I began letting out long, racking sobs, trying not to be too loud and alert someone. That would make everything worse. My face was red raw from my attempts to stop the never-ending tears. I tried my best to keep everything in, but failed miserably. It's not like I had nothing to cry over. My life was ruined, and it wasn't even my fault. I wouldn't be able to do anything I wanted and I could do nothing about it. Instead, I would be faced with the same four, carelessly painted walls forever. The same door and the same musty mattress. The same damp clothes. The same stale food. Everything will be the same. Apart from one singular thing, and arguably the most important. My life.

~

"Innocent."

Was I dreaming or was this really happening? Was I being taunted by a world that only existed in me? No, it couldn't be. Surely not.

Yet it was, and the smile that spread across my face went from ear to ear.

I was back in court for a third time, this time with the news I had been hoping for. The jury finally saw through his pathetic lies and instead saw the hidden truth. He was to blame, not me, and the months I had spent in a dirty cell were completely undeserved. When the verdict came through, I honestly wanted to break down into tears, but not like last time, this time happy ones. Slowly bending down, it took a few overwhelming moments to compose myself, struggling, but managing to stop the tears welling up in my eyes from falling down my cheeks. Looking down at my hands, I noticed they were shaking ever so slightly. I held them tightly together, in hopes of stopping them, but that only made my arms shake. Everything I wanted to happen had happened, and this time I wasn't dreaming. I wasn't going to wake up and face the disappointment that I had dreamt it all.

This time it was real. And I had been set free.

~

Before long, I was faced with the same green door I had missed for the past 5 months. Taking a deep, shaking breath, I started walking down the path, my thoughts going 100 miles an hour and feeling like I was on autopilot.

Today was a nice day with the sun beaming down on me and the sky dotted with white, fluffy clouds like candyfloss. The leaves of the neighbours' bush brushed up against my legs and a soft trace of pollen was left behind as I made my way towards the door. It was calling me, and I had to answer. Glancing into the front garden, I noticed the floor was littered with apples from the tree, some in perfect condition, some with small worm holes and some completely eaten to the core. I laughed to myself; I hadn't realised they would still grow fine unattended.

Minutes later, I was at the door. I felt my heartbeat speed up ever so slightly. I lifted my hand cautiously, and when it connected with the handle, I felt at ease. Sparks of electricity spread through me and I truly felt alive again, happy.

I was home.

BREAKOUT

By Wilbur Griffiths

The storm had arrived.

Waves the size of buses crashed onto the beaches of the remote Atlantic island. Lightning shot down from the heavens and taunted trees. And in the centre of the island, rain thundered down on the Turtle Bay Holding Centre, the most secure prison in the world. With 10-ft high walls of bedrock, 24-hour guard patrol and three control towers that saw everything in the prison, it was essentially a fortress.

No one could get in, and no one could get out.

At least, that was the plan. Cold, brutal reality came in that night and changed everything people thought about the penitentiary.

At the time that it happened, just one guard was alone on surveillance duty. This guard preferred not to have a name, and because of his surly manner and tendency not to talk, he didn't really have any friends - but he didn't care. All he cared about was making sure the prisoners didn't escape, which he was doing now from the perimeter wall. As he looked in through the tiny, bulletproof windows, he couldn't help but *want* someone to try and break out, for something interesting to happen. But everything was normal, and the guard was left deeply disappointed.

Halfway to the guard towers, he got his wish.

Talking into his radio: "Yes? What is it?"

"We have some... bad news. Some of the prisoners seem to be escaping and we need you to go-"

The guard already knew what the operator was going to say next. Swearing, he put down his radio and began to run over to the main entrance. Great big puddles of water burst open as he raced along the wall. It was very rare when a prisoner tried to escape, and even rarer when they *did*. And every time it happened, it was a pain in the neck. He just wished that this time it would be easy, and the prisoners would just give up. But then again, when had that ever happened?

Finally, he reached the end of the wall and ran down the stairs to join the 17 other patrollers waiting at the gate. He managed to squeeze past them into his spot at the very centre of the group, and checked all of his equipment. Taser? *Check*. Gun? *Check*. Radio? ...*not that I'll need it, but check*. He gave a brief sigh of relief as the head guard moved to the front to tell everyone the situation.

"All right everyone. There are three prisoners who believe they can escape by bribing the guards into their freedom. As the security of this prison, we will…"

The head guard's speech drifted over the guard's head. *Why today?* he thought to himself. *Of all the nights they could have picked to try and escape, it had to be today, the last day of me guarding the prison. Any other day I would have been fine, but I suppose we can't have everything.*

"…and so that's how they will be stopped today. Everyone understand?"

The guard snapped back into reality and nodded his head. He had no idea what to do, and was pretty worried about the outcome of the situation, but there was no getting out of this.

But as the gates opened, and everyone started marching in, he told himself to calm down. He had done this before. It was the same plan every time, same people every time and the same outcome every time - so why should he be worried? Nothing bad was going to happen.

The doors of the prison burst open with a loud bang and the guards stormed in. They were ready to execute their plan and stop the prisoners from escaping. They were ready for anything.

But what they had not expected was something that was lying in front of them right now:

Nothing.

There were no prisoners. No movement, no sounds, no sign that this even housed people, yet alone prisoners. It was the first silence that the prison had known in over a decade, to anyone and everyone standing there, it instantly felt like something was wrong.

To the guard of our story, the silence transformed the penitentiary into something new altogether. It used to be full of noise, and even though that noise was sometimes not the most reassuring thing to hear, he had grown accustomed to it; now the prison was deadly quiet, and the fact that every sound echoed around the room, and every footstep was a crash of thunder - it was enough to put him out of his comfort zone. He shuddered as the words of the commander boomed in his ears, but tried not to let anyone see. He *was* an officer, after all.

The next thing they did was try the dining room - same thing. No one was there, not even the person who served the food. The strange thing was that the prisoners were meant to be having their evening meal when the guards came in, but there was no sign of that. All the plates were spotless, the cutlery was unused and even the food in the serving trays were full. All of this made everyone very confused, but the longer that they spent examining every detail, the more time the prisoners had to escape.

This left just one room left: the cells themselves. It was very unlikely that the prisoners were in there, based on what had happened examining the previous rooms, but there was still a chance. By now the guard was very bored. Nothing had happened. At all. All he'd done was search a few rooms and examined a bowl of mushy peas. Chances were the prisoners weren't in there.

But still all the guards went through the doors, into the

room. There was no sign of any prisoners in there, but there were plenty of places to hide. They began scouting out all the possible places where they might be, not paying attention to anything else.

No-one saw the doors close behind them.

It was the guard that saw them first. Dressed in black and grey jumpsuits, which were far too big for them, peering out at the other guards looking all around, the prey watching the predators. But, as our guard realised, soon to be the other way round. They were going to get the jump, to distract them and run to freedom. He turned around to face the others, about to shout that they were here.

And that was when they made their move.

All hell broke loose. No-one, not even the prisoners, knew where anyone was, what to do, or where to go. All anyone knew was that there was a fight, and anyone could win.

The guards tried to use their tasers to stun the prisoners first, but they used iron bars to deflect the electricity, mostly onto other guards. Using their guns would be too risky, they decided. But fortunately for them, they knew how to use their fists. This was a move that the prisoners had not been expecting, and it took them a good minute to formulate a new plan, during which about a quarter of the prisoners had been knocked out (there were a *lot* of prisoners). They started using their fists to overpower the guards, too. And from there it transformed into a free-for-all fistfight.

By now the guard was very worried. The prisoners' plan was working. Everyone was distracted trying to get the enemy down on the ground, and absolutely no-one was watching the exit. But then again, none of the prisoners were trying to escape. Had his theory been wrong? As he tried to decide if they were going to run outside or not, a large force suddenly slammed into him, knocking him to the floor. Rubbing his head, he spun to his front to see an especially large prisoner staring down at him, his foot poised to strike into his side. In a flash, he rolled to one side and heard the swish of air as the boot swung through what had been his body a second ago. He scrambled to his feet, and for a few seconds, they both glared at each other, the sounds of the fight echoing in both their ears. Then the guard pulled out his taser and jabbed it at the other person. Of course, that other person pulled out an iron bar to deflect the electricity, but the guard had a plan. As the electricity touched the rod, his free hand grabbed the end of the bar that the prisoner was holding, and swung it towards their head. Two thousand volts of electricity exploded through him, and he immediately slumped in front of the guard. As he wiped sweat from his brow, he saw a few of the prisoners dash towards the door. Immediately he spun around and gave chase after them, no-one noticing he was even leaving in the chaos of the fight.

"STOP!" the guard shouted at the prisoners, but his words were lost in the screeching of the wind and the thudding of the rain outside. As they turned round a corridor, the guard slipped on a tray that had been left on the floor from earlier, and he crashed into the salad bar. Instantly, pain shot through him and a single cry left his mouth at the agony coursing through his leg. He had never experienced this much pain before; it felt like he could never get up again. And yet, through gritted teeth and shaking nerves, he stood up and began to chase once more.

By the time he got outside, the prisoners had… vanished. They couldn't have just disappeared into thin air - or could they? He tried to look round for them, but between the perimeter walls blocking his view and the aches in his ankle, he couldn't concentrate on anything. It didn't help that the rain had gotten seriously worse as well; if he'd thought it was bad when he had started, it was nothing compared to now. Nothing could be seen in this area, absolutely nothing. He tried scanning around the mud for footprints, but there were no signs of anything. Groaning with frustration, the guard was about to walk back to the prison when a clinking sound echoed underneath his feet.

Surprised, he looked down to find a shard of glass that was randomly lying on the floor. About two metres away lay another shard. Then, another two metres away, another. And another. The guard smiled to himself as he began to follow the fragments. It would appear he had found where the prisoners had gone.

The glass pieces led through the forest of the island and around the coast for some time, the guard observed.

This was very annoying for him, as it was hard for him to run down the track and dodge all the fallen trees at the same time. Eventually he got there, albeit panting and after 5 minutes. Just before reaching the end of the path, he crouched down, ready to activate his plan. He had been devising a theory that the prisoners had built a boat, based on other information he'd learnt when scanning the island a few months earlier. Tonight, he was going to ambush them just before they left on the boat, then arrest them and bring them back to the prison. As he was thinking to himself what the reward for capturing them was going to be, a rustling noise caught his attention. Instantly, he spun out from behind the bush, gun in one hand and taser in the other, ready to attack - then his eyes caught hold of the scene. This particular scene had a good side and a bad side. The good news was that he was right: they had been building a boat to escape.

The bad news was that they had just left the shore.

For a few seconds, all the guard did was stare as the boat began to head out to sea. Then his instincts kicked in and he charged towards it. Just from looking he could tell that he wasn't going to make it in time. As a last attempt to stop them, he pulled out his gun and started shooting. While one of his shots did hit one of them, they eventually got out of his range - and then all he could do was watch as the boat slowly sailed out of his view.

They were gone.

The words echoed around his brain as the guard sank to his knees. They were *gone*. Three prisoners. Escaped from the highest-security prison ever. And it was his fault. All too soon, the other guards would come and find him, and once they figured out what had happened, it was over for him. He'd be the laughing stock

And yet... and yet in a way he felt happy as well. Happy that he was going to finally leave after being stuck on an island for three years. Happy that he would be able to try new experiences and get out of the mind-set he'd had recently. And, most importantly he realised, happy for those three prisoners, who had finally experienced that same taste of freedom.

FLYING

By Aisha Quddus

It's cold, she thought, flinching at a gentle touch of the rippling water.

Her body shivered from a soft breeze that lingered in the thin air, causing her to hug her knees firmly whilst sitting on the frozen, solid edge of the dancing liquid. A strong smell of 'saltiness', that had accompanied the family since their arrival, had started making her feel slightly nauseous. Occasional splashes that surged from the rapid waters fell into the child's gentle eyes, causing an irritating sting. She removed her hands from comfort and began to furiously swipe her eyes with the sides of her warm knuckles.

She wished to go home. She never wanted to come here in the first place.

She waved towards her mummy and older sister, who were sitting along the stairs leading into the shallow pool, chatting about things the young girl didn't understand, but that wasn't much of a bother to her. She simply felt an urge to gain their attention, and failed miserably.

Before she could even yell, a large yet tame wave crossed her path, brushing against her chilled feet. She glanced in the direction of the unnatural current and spotted her father, who glided effortlessly in the hazy blue water. She believed it was done on purpose, yet pretended not to notice despite interest creeping into her mind. How surprised she was to see how easily he swam in the rushing water, reaching each end of the deep pool in under a minute.

It was like he was flying! And she wanted to fly too!

She didn't really hesitate, forgetting her previous complaints, and instead made her way to the calm and shallow end of the pool. She dipped her toes into the water, realising that it was noticeably warmer now. She wasted no time enveloping herself in her own curiosity.

The soft waves swept everywhere around her, and it was wonderful. The water level tickled her pale neck. She lifted her arm and observed the gentle water weighing down slightly on it like a thick blanket. She then took a few steps, occasionally stumbling like a baby giraffe. '*It's like moving in honey*', she thought as she noted the resistance of the heavy water. She soon became mobile, enjoying the weird feeling of the slight movements in the middle of the intriguing pool. Shortly after, she inspected the other swimmers, all absorbed in their own thing. She, too, wanted to do the same.

She was a little confused about how to begin, but briefly held her breath and ducked her head, fully engulfing herself in the spirited waters. It would be a lie to say she wasn't frightened, but that soon evaporated after she was distracted by the gentle splashes she had created. She lifted her legs, disconnecting herself unsteadily from the solid ground, but eventually balancing herself thanks to the plastic bands around her small arms. She remained still, staring at the far ground, reflecting on the numerous times she had fumbled before getting to where she was now.

And it soon got to her. That she was floating. She was flying!

OUR GREAT ESCAPE

By Ella Dent

We woke up. Our last day.

All our months of planning had led us to today; it was now or never.

We had found a blind spot in the CCTV coverage; we had spent weeks gathering all our equipment in secret, as well as days shovelling out the ground from under the fence to create a small gap almost big enough to fit a person. It all led to today.

We swallowed our lunch whole and went straight off to work. We were only 3 minutes into opening up the hole in the fence when our lookout signalled to us. Someone was coming. We dropped all of our stuff into the surrounding bushes. I gave a frantic look to another inmate. We had to make a run for it, or we would be seen. We could hear our lookout desperately trying to distract the person approaching. We knew we didn't have much longer

"1, 2, 3," I whispered.

Without looking back, we ran and ran and ran so far that even if the approaching member of staff had seen us they would have long lost track of us by now. We waited a couple of minutes, then a cold feeling of dread spread over my whole body as we made our way over to our construction site. What if this had all been for nothing? My heart was beginning to sink, I could barely face the thought of going back to how it used to be here: a hopeless cage that sucked the life out of all of us.

Even if this did all turn out to be for nothing, at least for two days the black and white walls had seemed brighter. We reached our destination. I breathed a sigh of relief; it was only then I realised I had been holding my breath the whole time.

We were all reunited back at our spot once the coast was clear, all except for our lookout. I still was not quite at ease. What had happened to our lookout? Had he told them what we were planning?

I had to push that all aside and focus on the task at hand. CLANG

We swing our shovels at the bottom of the fence in order to increase the small tunnel space so that it became big enough for all of us to fit through. A cluster of butterflies beat around in my stomach, more and more with each swing. We were so close. I could almost taste the sweet air of the outside world.

Finally we had broken though. We had done it!

The whistle blew. I decided we should escape later that day with the cover of night when everyone was asleep. It would give us the chance to get back to our cell and grab the few measly possessions we had and wanted to keep.

That night, after we were allowed back up to our cell, we were all buzzing with excitement. We were hurriedly packing all our stuff into a pillowcase when suddenly the door opened. The sound made me jump out my skin. I was already on edge from the fear of being caught. Our lookout entered. He had told the guards that he was going for a walk and got lost. They couldn't get anything else out of him but they still suspected something out of the ordinary was going on.

"I'm worried they might look again tomorrow and find us," he stuttered with great concern and worry in his eyes.

"Don't worry, we will be long gone by then," I smiled.

We sneaked out of our cell carefully, precise as a watchmaker with our movements, to not attract any unwanted attention.

I have been here for 4 years and I have become quite familiar with the guards' patrol patterns but it was going to be hard. We snaked around corners with me leading the rest of the small pack of inmates. We made it outside and over to our spot, the cool, peaceful night air calming my racing heart a little.

I was anxious to see whether our small tunnel under the fence would still be there. Subconsciously, some of me must have wondered if this had all been a crazy dream.

I turned on a flashlight and the compound around us lit up; the other inmates followed turning on their flashlights too and we began to navigate around the tight corners and complex turns. It felt almost like the beginning of a horror movie: the dead of night, the black sky only kept alive by the dull white flickering of our flashlights; complete silence apart from our echoing footsteps, as well as the slow drip, drip, drip of water hitting the floor from the buildings above.

After what seemed like forever, we finally reached our destination. My heart skipped a beat. There it was in front of me: freedom itself!

I climbed through first. It was tight but I managed. One by one, our small cohort of inmates crawled through the small gap under the fence.

I stood up and patted the dirt off my clothes, soaking up the moment, tasting the sweet air, feeling the cool breeze passing over my face, the feeling of freedom. We had done it. We were free.

We ran, and we never looked back. We had escaped our boarding school.

ABOUT THE AUTHORS

The writers of this anthology are all students from The Priory School, across years 7-11. This is the second anthology produced by the school but this collection features a range of new authors. The book anthology club was set up to celebrate creative writing and to raise the profile of reading and writing in the school to celebrate World Book Day 2022.

The Priory School is a co-educational secondary school and sixth form located in Hitchin in the English county of Hertfordshire. The Priory School is the only co-educational secondary school in Hitchin.

More Titles From The Priory School you might like:

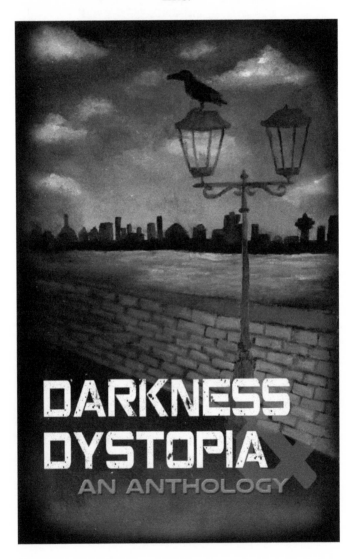

Lightning Source UK Ltd.
Milton Keynes UK
UKHW040651030322
399515UK00001B/213